Dedicated to the students of Centennial Lane Elementary School,
including all of the children in this story,
especially E, F, I, K, M, O, P, Q, and my three Ms.
—A.H.D.

To the neighborhood friends I've made over the years.
Without you, the bus stop would not be as fun.
—L.W.

Text © 2022 Angela H. Dale
Illustrations © 2022 Lala Watkins

Book design by Melissa Nelson Greenberg

Published in 2022 by CAMERON + COMPANY, a division of ABRAMS

Library of Congress Cataloging-in-Publication Data available.
ISBN: 978-1-951836-47-4

Printed in China

10 9 8 7 6 5 4 3 2 1
CAMERON KIDS is an imprint of CAMERON + COMPANY

CAMERON + COMPANY
Petaluma, California
www.cameronbooks.com

BUS STOP

by **ANGELA H. DALE**   illustrated by **LALA WATKINS**

cameron kids

Sleepy street.
Still.
Gray.
Empty bus stop.

School day.

Antoine arrives.

Beatrice burrows.
Carlos catches.
Divya drifts.

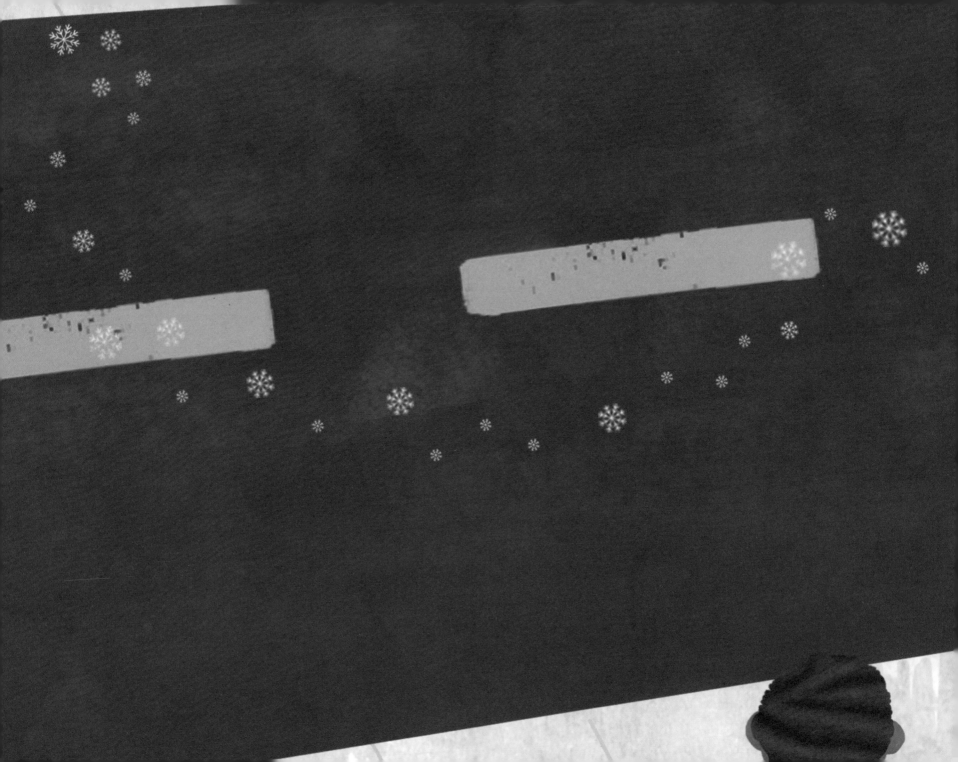

The bus will be here soon.

Emmy scouts.
Fran sketches.
Griffin skips.

No bus yet.

Hannah stomps.
Isaiah romps.

Joelle waltzes.
Kartik wonders:
Where's the bus?

Lyric leaps.

Mahmoud laughs.

Nina lags.
She is late.

But the bus is later.

Orion scoops.

Polly stoops.

Quinn whoops.

Still no bus.

Little Riya reports:

nooooSc

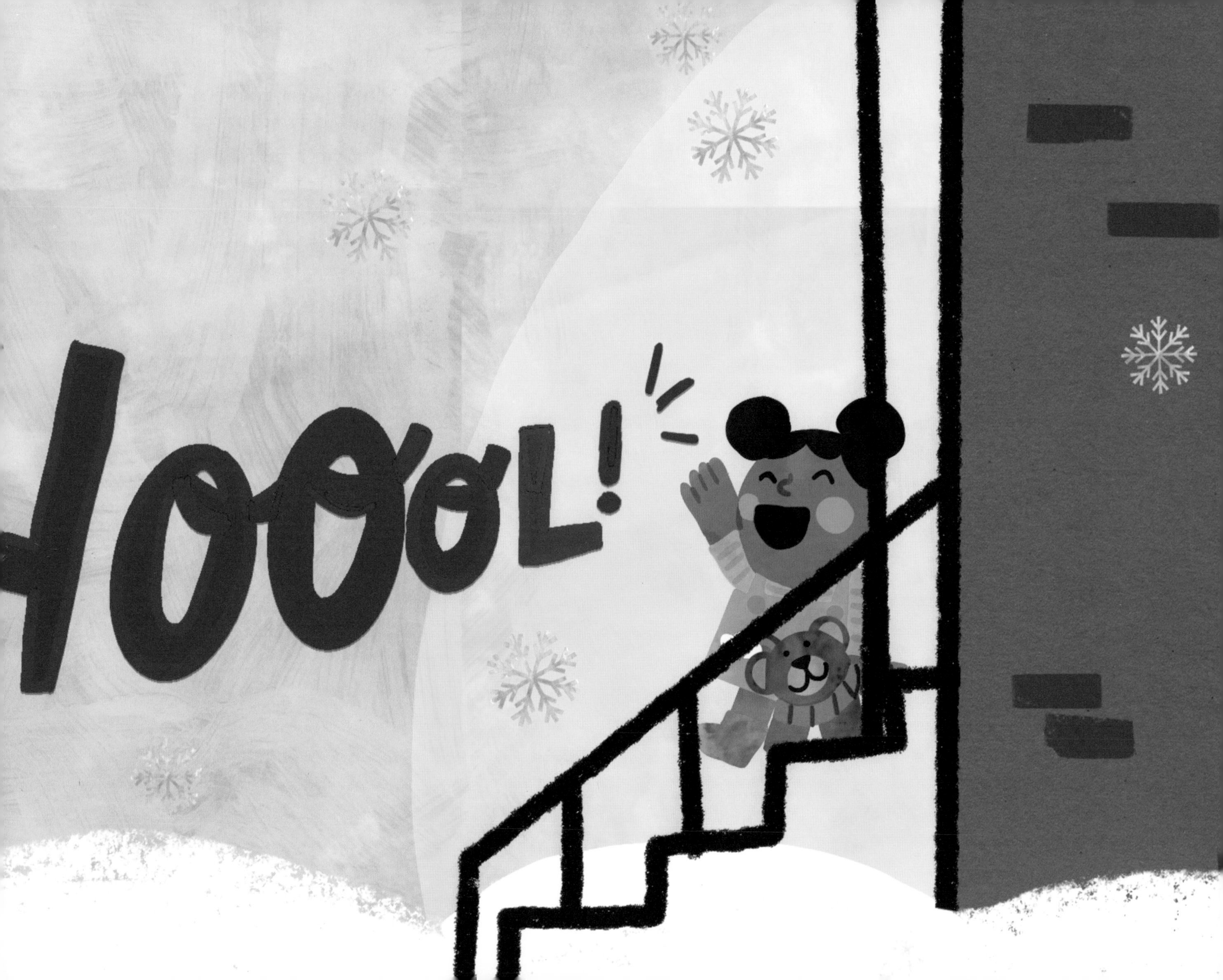
HOOOL!

Sofia flaps.
Tyshawna flies.
Umer rolls.
Victor slides.
Wyatt whirls.
Ximing spins.
Yoshi cheers.
Zoey grins.

Empty bus stop.
Thrill.
Play.
Swirling street.

Snow day!